Flight of the Black Butterfly

Shawn Savoie

Flight of the Black Butterfly

Published in Hampton, VA, by Fruition Publishing Concierge Services™. Fruition Publishing Concierge Services is a division of Alesha Brown, LLC.

Fruition Publishing Concierge Services™ can bring authors to your live event. For more information or to book an event, visit Fruition Publishing Concierge Services™ at:

www.FruitionPublishing.com

ISBN: 978-1-954486-44-7 Paperback

ISBN: 978-1-954486-45-4 eBook

Library Of Congress Control Number: 2022907626

Contents

Dedication

To my mama (Priscilla M. McKnight), who taught me how to love.

To my mother (Crystal D. Jones), who taught me how to conduct myself while being in love.

They endured pain and scars so that they could pass down wisdom and valuable lessons to me. From these two amazing women, I learned that many of us become impatient when waiting for love. Sometimes we tell ourselves that we will go out into the world to find our true love.

The truth is we are not Cupid. Only God

orchestrates true love. Through God's eyes, life is a flight of stairs. People are going up. People are going down. It's not about who's going up or down. The only thing that matters is that we arrive at our destination.

Sometimes God uses his hands to elevate us. They are elevators that take us right where he wants us. Once we reach our destination, we either fall in love or land in a place where we get prepared to be loved. God makes no mistakes.

Handsome Is His Name

Oh, my diary, I met a handsome guy today
I was mesmerized by his eyes
It was like looking through a telescope and
seeing where the moon goes while the sun
lights the sky.

His skin shined like particles of sand when the
light hit them
Like SWV, my knees became weak
I tried to tell him my name but
I could not speak.

His smile made my insides melt
I felt my heart dissolve into one big puddle
of love
Maybe this is love at first sight.
He's all I'm thinking of.

I'm so glad he gave me his number
Now he's a call away
I may call today, but I don't want my eagerness
to run him away.

Bonding Time

I'm loving this moment
Us walking and talking
Just he and I
We meet at the park just before the sun shuts
its eye.

Colors ooze across the sky
He entertains the child within me
He chases me and watches me go down slides
I sway back and forth on a horsey ride.

He pushes me on park swings
We do things, after-dark things, like taste the
sweetness of each other's lips
This is a moment I don't want to end
I want to press my lips against his again and
again.

Caking

When butterflies are in my stomach, it's hard to keep still
I'm not sure what to call this feeling that I feel.

When we first began talking on the phone, I was in the room
After that, I was in the kitchen dancing with the broom.

I even found myself sitting out in the car
Soon after, I was lying across the kitchen bar.

Shawn Savoie

I made my way to the closet
I even graced the bathroom mirror with
my face
I found myself moving and dancing all over the
place.

The time came and went like the wind
I talked in every part of the house tonight
Next, I'll be on the roof next to the satellite.

On My Mental

I can't take my mind off of him
He lives rent-free inside of my mind
He's on every floor
He's behind every door
I love having him as a tenant
He makes me laugh, smile, and blush
This rush of emotions knock me off of my feet
like waves
I see him everywhere I go, but it's only my
mind playing tricks on me
His words stick on me like pollen on bees
How else could he run through my mind this
much?

Shawn Savoie

18

Could It Be Love

Is this love that I'm feeling?
Like a basketball, my heart bounces inside my
chest cavity
My blood rushes through my veins like raging
waters
My mind only thinks of him
My eyes only see him
I skipped breakfast twice this week
Maybe I'm living off of love
He made his way into my dreams
I hear his voice when he's not around
His gentle touch turns my stomach the way
roller coasters do

Shawn Savoie

I like the things he's dealing
Maybe this is the love that I'm feeling.

Say It

Tell me you feel the same way I do
Tell me so I can stop wondering and hiding
what I feel
Say that love makes your heart move
It makes your heart groove like people dancing
to music
Say that love brings forth visions of the future
It allows you to see dates and quality time that
we haven't experienced yet
For me, love does that and so much more
I hope love does that for you
It's amazing the things that love do.

Shawn Savoie

Sofa Sitting

The silence is much louder than the TV
We see romantic gestures in the movie that
makes us lessen the space between us
His left arm rests on my shoulders, and my left
hand rests on his thigh
To keep me warm, he wraps me in his arms
His heartbeat vibrates my shoulders
When he exhales, the breeze tickles my ear
Something in the atmosphere has our hearts
pounding uncontrollably fast
It's as if they are dying to burst out of our
chests so they can meet each other
While the clock ticks and tocks, our eyes lock
Just wondering what the other is thinking.

Shawn Savoie

24

Pleasurable Pain

My body is burning and throbbing from your
touch
You're watching my figure slither like a snake
I'm watching your hands glide across my skin
We're watching everything except the television
It's hard to resist the urge
I'm dying to let our bodies merge like water
droplets
We shall move and flow as one
I don't know how you take control of me
I once heard someone say that nothing is open
after midnight except for legs
That must be true because my legs are shaped
like the letter V.

Shawn Savoie

Deep Kind Of Love

I have let you close to my heart
I have told you secrets that only walls know
I'm trying to fall slowly, but I'm gravitating to
you quickly.

I know I said I love you first
If you ever want to be in love, we can fall into it
together
We'll just fall right in it.

We'll spend tonight in it and every night after
this one
I love you now, tomorrow, and forever.

Shawn Savoie

We may fall out crying
We may fall out laughing
But I hope we never fall out of love.

Proud Love

When I love, I love out loud
I let it show
I let my friends and co-workers know.

I change my relationship status on social
media
I even upload pictures of us.

When you love me, love me out in the open
Give me public affection
Hold my hand
Make your hugs tight
Give me the same attention you give me at
night.

Shawn Savoie

You know how you look at me like
I'm the only girl in the world?
Let's do things like no one is looking.

Lasting Love

If life is truly what we make it
I want our lives to be long and lasting like a
river
May our love forever flow like the mighty
Mississippi.

Let's do what makes us happy
Things that will make us crack a smile so wide
that camera lenses can't capture it.

As long as we're happy, nothing else matters
This is more than food for thought
This is poetic gumbo.

Shawn Savoie

I hope your appetite for love and happiness is
as big as Dumbo
We'll be full of love, full of life, and full of peace.

Where Are You?

Come out wherever you are
I'm looking for the man I fell in love with
The man that's here now got to be a clone
The man I once knew would never treat me
this way
He wouldn't leave me here all alone.

Communication isn't the same
He doesn't speak my love languages
Maybe after playing hide and seek with
demons, he became trapped behind a door in
his mind.

Maybe he's playing a joke on me
It's not even April, and he's trying to fool me.

I hope to recognize my love again
I want to see the love in his eyes
I want to feel the passion in his hands
I need to see everything he promised me.

Inquiring Mind

My intuition is rattling my spirit
I even hear it whispering through my ear
canals
It alerts me when something isn't right and
tonight is that night.
His hug smells like his sweat, his cologne, and
a perfume that's not mine.
That's not fine because my mind won't allow me
to rest until I find answers.
Who was close enough to leave their scent
on him?
Who does he hug tighter and longer than me?
Who is comfortable enough to touch him the
way I do?

It's not fair having more questions than
answers
It makes me feel crazy.

Competing with Technology

Getting to know someone was once a trial of great simplicity until technology complicated bonding.

Take me back to the funny days when he and I laughed, talked, and walked on sunny days.

Our mouths transformed words into sentences, and our minds turned those sentences into images.

Nowadays, when I want to talk, texting is his choice of communication.

Take me back to that late night
It was our first date night, and we created
magical moments.

I laughed so hard that I felt a tingle in my
funny bone
He gave me a kiss that was sweeter than a
honeycomb.

These days, video games and social media get
more attention from him than I do
Take me back to the days when he said he
would never let me go.

He said that he would never let me go
That's what he told me
Now he holds his phone and controller more
than he holds me.

Love Taps

When my man loves me, he loves hard
I can feel his love throughout my entire body.

I find it seeping out of my eyes
His love bounces and rings inside of my ears
I feel it throbbing in my chest
His love is all over my face.

When his love taps me, I feel it
Nothing can erase it, and nothing can heal it.

When his love taps me, everyone knows it
Scars remind them, and bruises show it.

Shawn Savoie

In the still of the night, I roam the hallways of
my mind just to find an exit door.
It hurts to face reality
I feel the type of pain that would make some
people cry oceans of tears.

I'm under pressure that would shatter some
people like cell phone screens
Love shouldn't hurt
Love shouldn't tap me.

Hereditary Pain

In my reflection, I see my mother
Maybe it's because my present is her history
I inherited her insomnia, broken heart, and
silent cries.

Just like her, I suffer in silence to avoid any
violence
Sleeping with a broken heart is better than
staying up all night picking up broken dishes.

Sometimes curiosity throws a party in my mind
It makes me so restless
Doubt, worry, and anxiety are all on the guest
list.

Shawn Savoie

Where is your boyfriend? They ask.
Why is he always late? They ask.
Why does he ignore your calls? They ask.
These are questions that I don't have
answers to.

To avoid arguments and violence
I suffer in silence.

How long can I muffle my cries?
I wish my mother were here to wipe my eyes.

Loner

Love me
Leave me
Same sad song
Go ahead and abandon me like everyone else
It's nothing new to me.

Some days I needed a father, but he needed
liquor because it was a quicker solution to
ending his pain.

Some days I needed a mother, but she needed
money because it made her smile
After a while, money didn't stay
It left and took her smile away.

Some days I needed a brother, but he needed
to live life fast and explore the vast streets to
find what he was missing.

Some days I needed a sister, but she needed a
mister to assist her on how to love.

Some days I needed someone just to be there,
but I learned we must stand alone to find out
how strong we really are.

I am mighty.

Fool In Love

When you said that you needed space
I didn't think you were talking about outer
space.

You left me on Jupiter feeling stupider than the
kid who ran to the stop sign after someone told
him that Christmas was around the corner.

I say Cupid is to blame
I was living my best life until he struck me with
his arrow that made me stumble and fall in
love.

Shawn Savoie

Before I got close to you, I was getting close
to God
Jesus and I were such good friends
We constantly talked on the mainline
I bet now he's wondering why I've missed so
many of his calls.

I now know why fools fall in love
Our big hearts makes us clumsy
As silly as it sounds, part of me misses you.

If I could, I would rewind time just to watch you
walk back into these arms of mine.

In some dreams, I've seen us on Venus
I somehow used the stars to depict our faces
just to give other couples something to look
up to.

Maybe my expectations were too high
I was a fool in love
I was a fool for you
The next time I fall in love, I hope it doesn't
hurt when I land.

Breakup

You told me to let you go
My hands listened, but my mind did not.

Here, deep in my mind, I play and rewind the
magical moments we created.

If only I knew what the lonely do when it's time
to start over.
Do they become clumsy and fall into a new
love?
How do they find a new walk?
How do they develop a new talk?

Shawn Savoie

Tomorrow and every day that follows will start
and end without you
Is this the forever you promised me?
Will I forever endure this pain?

Magic Show

Ladies, beware of the great magician and his
power
He's only able to shapeshift into Mr. Right after
you've told him about the man of your dreams
It feels perfect and divine, but everything is not
as it seems.

He fills your mind with such beautiful illusions
All of your wishes, dreams, and hopes seem
close enough to touch
His hold on you is powerful
In reality, he injures you emotionally and
mentally so that he can be your crutch.

Shawn Savoie

After indulging in your fruit of passion, he
transforms into his true self
Beware of the great magician.

He comes promising happiness but leaves you
in sorrow
Watch him perform his great disappearing act
Here today and gone tomorrow
He's on to his next performance.

Liar Liar

Men tell many and plenty of lies:
"I'm going to rock your world.
I will give you the world.
I won't hurt you."

They can't rock our worlds
The only thing that's rocking is their pea-sized
brain inside of that super dome on top of their
shoulders.

They can't give us the world because their
hands aren't big enough
They promise to never hurt us, but in the end,
the pain they inflict feels like salt on wounds.

Shawn Savoie

The lies men tell sound poetic:
"I am incomplete without you.
You're the better half that makes me whole.
You are my everything."

Men come to us whole
They're a whole problem
How can we be their everything if they put
every other thing before us?

Men tell many and plenty of lies
Read between the lies men tell.

Trust Issues

I once had that blind trust
That never mind trust because I was all his and
he was all mine.

Now I don't trust any man as far as I can throw
an anchor
Lies are premeditated
Lies hurt.

Lie, lie, lie
That's all they know
That's all they do
Lie to me and lie to you.

Shawn Savoie

No matter how you word them
All lies cause pain
I find it funny how men promise to never hurt
women until life arranges situations to remind
them they shouldn't make promises they can't
keep.

At times I want to weep
Just cry myself a river filled with all my sorrow
so I can sail into a better tomorrow.

No man should ever knock on the door of my
heart
I won't give them the key
There's no love here
There's nothing inside of me.

Have you seen her?

I'm looking for this woman
Has anyone seen her?
Take some flyers and pass them down
Pass them around.

Look at the light inside of her eyes and smile
Just look at how her skin glows
If anyone knows where she is, please tell me or
just let her know that she's deeply missed.

I need her to come back home
I've been searching for this lady high and low
I wait on leads that will let me know which way
to go.

Shawn Savoie

If anyone happens to see this woman
Tell her I'm waiting
I will be waiting in the last place I saw her.

I shall wait in the bathroom mirror, hoping to
see her smile once more
I'm waiting for the person I was before I
allowed the wrong men into my life.

Prayers From Room 306

Dear Heavenly Father
Oh thou that control the Heavens and Earth
I beg of thy mercy.

There is a fear buffet in this place
These rooms feed on our fear of the unknown
It is what keeps the lights on in this place.

No longer will I put my trust in these doctors
who claim to be healers
They're just modern-day drug dealers.

Medicine is either too addictive or temporarily
works.

Shawn Savoie

Oh, dear father
I have doubt, fear, and anxiety
Like parasites, they leach on my insides and
drain my energy slowly.

Please take them out of me
Once they make it out of me, hopefully, I will
have enough strength to fight.

I want to fight for another day
Fight for a brighter future
I am not finished yet
I have yet to give birth.

I pray that someday you bless me with an earth
angel
I have yet to cross paths with my king
I want a man that will share me with you.

Please, oh Lord
Please make a way
Take away all that hinders me from walking out
of this place.

Lupus Warrior

I know you want to crush my spirit the way
tides crush sandcastles
I know you're enjoying my suffering.

Fluctuate my weight
Damage my skin
Take away my hair
Take away my warmth
But you will never take away my will to fight.

I'm sure you want me to give up
I know you want to see me in tears.

Shawn Savoie

Shoot your pain all over my body
Make it feel as if I'm walking on broken glass
or needles
Stiffen all of my joints
But I will not fall.

I will defeat you, Lupus
I will win
Victory will be mine.

Diamonds Are A Girl's Best Friend

Just like us women, they undergo pressure and
heat that changes them
We both know how important it is to be hard in a
world that breaks you
We both know what it feels like to be only a
trophy to most men
We've known each other all too well for a very
long time
We will be the best of friends until the end of time
Men only recognize our paralyzing beauty
We will never be easily broken
We get reshaped
We get cut
We last.

Shawn Savoie

Damaged Goods

I am not yet ready
My poor future soulmate
I hope he's not out there searching for me
He will never find me until I find myself.

I'm currently somewhere between surrendering
and persevering
I don't know which way to go
I gave men all of me, and they left without
reciprocating all the love I gave them.

Love, as I know it, has no happy ending
It's far from a fairytale
Those clowns always have the last laugh.

Shawn Savoie

Love is a carnival that I know very well
There are wild rides we know as emotional
rollercoasters and mood swings.

Sometimes I feel like a hand-me-down
Just used goods hoping to do the next person
some good.

At times, caterpillars give me hope
If they can change and start a new life, then I
can have a new start as well.

One day I'll be made over
Someday, I will transform into the queen
I am called to be.

No Take Backs

Hey there, ex
How may I help you?
You're such a blast from the past
You left my feelings all over the place.

I cleaned up your mess
I fixed everything you broke
You may pry, and you may poke, but you will
never enter my world again.

A part of me knew that you would return to me
thirsty
Luckily for you
I bottled every tear that you made me cry.

I hope they make you feel the way you made
me feel
I want them to remind you of the pain I
endured.

Drink up
Let these tears conjure memories of the pain
you caused me
Drink up
Leave the bottle empty the same way you
left me.

The Side Effect of Loneliness

Watch out for the hands of loneliness
Don't let them push you into the arms of
bad men.
Look out for the feet of loneliness
They will kick you out of your peaceful place.

Don't listen to the voice of loneliness
She will try to convince you that you're missing
something.
Never look into the eyes of loneliness
She will only show you that no one is at your
side.

Shawn Savoie

Don't answer when loneliness knocks
You will realize that misery truly loves company.
Doing things out of loneliness will only leave
you lonely
It will leave you empty like an alcoholic's bottle.

Loneliness is a time for self:
Self-reflection
Self-love
Self-esteem
Self-care.

All Eyes On Me

All eyes on me
Green, blue, brown, and hazel
Some men have to be dreaming if they think
that I can be bought.

I make my own money
Oh, how I wish men could buy manners with a
reality check.

All eyes on me
Green, blue, brown, and hazel
Hey guys, if y'all can't hold an intelligent
conversation, then y'all can't get my attention.

Shawn Savoie

If y'all can't get my attention, then y'all can't
hold my hand
You all are incapable of grasping the simple
things, but y'all expect to hold my body.

All eyes on me
Green, blue, brown, and hazel
Goodbye guys
I'm fine, y'all see
Never mind me.

I have enough friends in my friend zone
I only have room in my life for a king
All eyes on me
Green, blue, brown, and hazel.

8 Dresses

I've walked at eight weddings
That's eight dresses
That's eight times I had to hide my
disappointment
Behind a smile.

When is it going to be my turn to be the bride?
I'm always the maid
Where is my king that was tailored by angels
just for me?

Maybe he will insert himself into my life
On a day when I need his aid.

Shawn Savoie

Often, I imagine how his proposal is going to
play out
Maybe he'll slip the ring on my finger while I
sleep
Maybe he will be on one knee outside my
house when I'm on my way out.

I hope he knows that it's my way or the highway
He just has to pay for everything and show up
on time.

I've only been planning my wedding since the
age of twelve
and nothing will ruin my moment
If I don't get married by a certain age, then
that's that
I'll be destined to live with a dog or a cat.

Hopes and Dreams

My love
My future king
I wish I could tell you that I've found love's
definition.

It came to me in a divine premonition where
you and I were lying in bed, refusing to eat
because we were living off love.

I hope you're still searching for me
I hope your determination to find me didn't die.

Shawn Savoie

My dreams of us are immortal
They serve as a portal to help me escape my
lonely reality.

Often, I pictured us cruising the road while the
sun's eye slowly closes
I sing my favorite song while you shout along,
and I tell you to hush because this is a solo.

If life ever aligns the road of fate so that you
and I could meet
You would no longer be the man of my dreams;
you would be my reality.

Sadly, you're still a dream to me
I'm your queen to be
I'm waiting for you to complete your quest
to me.

A Place Called Peace

I have finally found peace
All my life, I thought peace was a feeling, but
peace is actually a place.
It's a place where I don't have to deal with
unprepared men
I don't have to worry about any attacks from
the enemy.

Peace is a place for members only
Admission is free
No baggage allowed.

I had to let go of anything that was slowing my
movement toward improvement.

Shawn Savoie

I let go of anxiety, doubt, grudges, and worry
when I found peace
My spirit went into do not disturb mode
If unbothered were a person, I would be it
Nothing will disturb my peace.

Woke

This is a farewell to the stubborn person I have become.

I say my heart is cold when it really feels like hot stones
I act like a mule when I'm really a unicorn.

Unprepared men have made me unprepared for my future king
I must gather myself and collect my thoughts.

I lost pieces of myself in bad relationships
I must rebuild with the rubble they left me with.

Shawn Savoie

No one will ever again lower my value by
damaging me
When I'm back on the market, my castle will
only be fit for a king.

Broken

I see that you're broken, madame, but I must
tell you that God gave me the ability to fix
anything.

Piece by piece, I will reassemble your heart
and bind every part with a promise to never
allow it to become broken.

I'm sure you've heard that promise before, but
you never heard it from my mouth
I refuse to break your heart or any promise
I want to touch you deeply without making love.

Shawn Savoie

I want you to know your naked truth without you
disrobing
Please don't fear falling for me because I vow
to catch you.

Yes, I know you've been caught before, but I
play for keeps
I shall catch and keep you in my life
I won't let go.

Message from the King

Who am I?
You ask
Well, I am your king.

If you are wondering how I know
My ancestors tell me so
They whisper to me in the winds
They visit me in dreams.

I walk with purpose and for a purpose
I come to you, my queen, not to make you
happy but to show you what it is like when
someone loves you back properly.

I am no wizard or sorcerer
I don't possess the power to make you happy,
but I have the courage to love even when I see
you have forsaken it.

Why do I call you queen, you ask?
I call you queen because that is what you are
and who you are.

You command the sun
Your skin refracts sunlight, which is why you
have this amazing glow about you.

If the heavens created anything more beautiful
than you
It must be too small to be seen by man.
When they ask who we are
We shall tell them that we're royalty.

We are the salt of the earth
The main ingredient
Without us, the melting pot would be bland.

Stand, my queen
Stand with me
Stand beside me
Stand for love.

Shawn Savoie

* * *

84

Resurrecting the Queen

Don't forget who you are
Please remember that before you were called
Baby, honey, or boo,
You were addressed as queen.

Birds envied your voice
Flowers swayed in the breeze just to
acknowledge your beauty.

The sun kissed you because it missed you
while it had to illuminate the other side of the
world
Your mere presence turned men into boys.

Shawn Savoie

Stand, my queen
I need you to rise
Rise like your hair in its natural state
Rise like every line in Maya Angelou's "Still I
Rise."
Rise like black power fists during the national
anthem in the 1968 Olympics.

I want you to thrive again
Look alive again.

Never forget that God made Eve for Adam,
which means Adam was definitely missing
something.

Searching for Love

Oh, my lost lady
I hope you didn't look for love in all the wrong
places on a daily basis.

Finding Mr. Right takes so long because Mr.
Wrong always distracts you and wastes your
time.

I bet others took your love and misused it or
confused it for something replaceable.

Shawn Savoie

Our time is near
My heart is here
My mind is clear
Maybe one day you'll see me here.

You don't have to wait or search anymore
Spare yourself the heartache by letting love
find you
When you turn around, I'll be right behind you.

I am waiting to show you what true and
unconditional love is.

Mental Tug Of War

Dear Diary
This new guy is very persistent
What does he want from me?

I'm difficult to catch like fireflies, and he's hard
to get rid of like roaches.

He approaches me with sweet words every
morning
That smile of his is bright and early like
the sun.

His almond brown skin has a glow to it
His aromatic cologne must be composed of
every flower there is.

He reminds me of my coffee that's strong but
sweet
My heart is so afraid of opening up, but my
mind says don't be.

Maybe he'll be my downfall, or maybe he
won't be
Maybe I can find a love that is strong enough
to suspend gravity.

I'll be high enough to grab a star out of the
night sky
Or I can allow fear to deprive me of love.

I can't help but imagine if he and I were
poured into a cup
We would be the world's best cup of tea
Sweet, strong, soothing, and therapeutic
I'm dying to try that tea.

High Hopes

To the woman that thinks she will never love
again
Many say that love never dies.

I hope your love gets resurrected as a rainbow,
and once I reach the other side
You'll be standing there with your heart of gold.

I know that you've been waiting on your Prince
Charming for so long that he's probably a
King now.

If hope truly floats
I want to place all my hope inside of you so you
will never have to drown in your own tears
again.

I hope to give you a reason to delete all of your
dating site accounts
I hope to give you a reason to conquer your
fear of falling so we can fall in this love
together.

I hope you know that I'm in this for the
long-run
Your past partners were sprinters, but I run
marathons.

Forever and ever, it will be us against the world
That means us versus them, her, and him
We shall deal with anyone who threatens our
love, peace, and happiness.

Taking A Gamble

Some say that love is a gamble
If that is true, then a part of me hopes that if I
play my cards right,
I can become the king of your heart.

Maybe we can be jokers
Just fools in love living off of love.

You should know that I dropped all of my bad
habits
So that I can catch you whenever you're ready
to fall for me.

Shawn Savoie

I hope I'm in your thoughts
I want to run through your mind until I feel the
burn in my legs.

I wish for us to make a connection like protons
and electrons
May we form a bond that can never be broken,
not even by time.

Yes, I know time is undefeated, but I would still
attempt to
Beat it just so we could have a slice of forever.

Our love will be as beautiful as those paintings
in the sky that we call sunsets.

A Chance at Romance

I see the real you, madame
I'm not talking about the Mona Lisa you are on
the outside
I'm speaking to the shattered woman on the
inside.

Change is all you need
Let me change your worldview as you change
my world too.

Shawn Savoie

I only wish to help you find the highest degree
of happiness so that you can smile without
being in front of a camera
You will laugh without a joke being told
That's a beautiful scene if you can picture it.

Hopefully, your mind can frame that photo in
your memory
I know you don't need me, but if need be
I can help you find this place we call peace.

Hopefully, curiosity badgers you with
persuasion day and night no matter the
occasion
I hope that your heart, mouth, and hands will
eventually tell me yes
I hope you take a chance at romance.

First Date

Picnic in the park
Our very first date
The warm summer breeze caresses our skin as
it passes by.

His cologne compels me to sit next to him
Our conversation flows smoothly like a river
I analyze his every word just to be sure it
matches everything he said over the phone.

His jokes, along with my laughter, weaken me
But I enjoy this pleasurable pain
Food and snacks silence us but don't stop our
mouths from moving.

Shawn Savoie

To remember the moment we immortalize
ourselves in pictures
Like kids, we lock eyes and chuckle
A raging cold wind blows as the sun hides
behind a cloud.

It's getting closer to sunset, but we're not
finished having fun yet
We stare at each other with one question
written all over our faces:
What's next?

First Kiss

Our tender lips meet
I find your sugar healthy
It moves all of me.

Shawn Savoie

Chillin

Parked car conversations
We talk about this and talk about that.

In the back of my mind, I hope I'm not being
loquacious
But I'm very talkative when I get nervous.

Good vibes
Good music
Good time.

Our warm breath gives us privacy by creating
condensation that fogs the windows
This moment is for our eyes only.

I'm unable to see the night sky, but that's
alright because I see stars in his eyes.

As our fingers interlock
I take a moment to count all one hundred and
fifty ridges of his fingerprint.

It's amazing what you can do when you live in
the moment
My heart pounds so fast and hard that the
pendant on my necklace bounces on my chest.

Our atmosphere is heated by the passion deep
inside of us
This passion amplifies our body heat and gives
us fever
I love the way it burns
Every song on the radio seems to conjure my
wild side.

We flirt with time as if we have all the time in
the world
But that's a lie because I have work in the
morning and
I need to tell him goodnight before I do
something that
I may regret.

Shawn Savoie

Make It Home

Red lights
Blue lights
My date and I were sitting in his car when the
cops approached us.

My heart fell in the pit of my stomach and
rattled my insides
Questions flooded my mind
Will we make it home tonight?
Are we going to jail?
Why were we approached?

What happens when a king lion and a hunter
have a standoff?
How can I pacify the anger of my date?
How can I save his black life and make him
believe that it matters to me?

When police stop you, they like to play a game
called "cop says"
If you make the wrong move, a bullet will end
the game.

So we refuse to participate in their game of
trickery
I don't reach for anything except for God as I
pray inside my head
I hope my prayers reach him
I pray that God allows us to make it home
tonight.

Trauma

If absence truly makes the heart grow fonder, I
will wander way over yonder until tranquility,
and I miss each other.

Oh, madame, I should tell you that this
distance between us has nothing to do with you
It has everything to do with my bad encounters
with the police.

On the inside, I'm a ticking bomb, and I would
hate for you to be in the blast radius when I
explode
Just the sight of a cop makes anger run
through my veins and boil my blood.

The first time some black women received
flowers was at their funeral
The first time some black men experienced a
peaceful sleep was after they were buried.

I'm tired of cops getting away with murder
I'm tired of tears moisturizing the face of black
mothers
I'm tired of black families planning more
funerals than weddings, parties, and
graduations.

Sometimes I want to travel to the darkest
region of my mind to unleash my animal side
I want to give oppressors a dose of their own
medicine and watch the side effects drive them
crazy.

Badges awaken my anger
Flashing lights trigger my anxiety
Seeing injustices makes me want to exercise
my rage.

Leap Of Faith

I need you to let go
Stop holding on to the past
Just let it go and fall.

I'm here hoping to convince you that you will
be in good hands like Allstate
I want to give you that Al Green type of love
and happiness after I mend your broken heart.

I can't guarantee that the rest of our time on
this earth will be pleasant, but I vow to treat
our time like water in a desert
I will cherish it and never waste it.

To be mine will feel amazing
I want you to feel like Wonder Woman and not
like a woman wondering if she can endure
more pain from villains.

I just want to see you smile as wide as my
wingspan
I only want to see you happy.

Vacancy

You said that your heart is vacant, my lady
That's great news because I've been searching
for a place to store my love.

Give me the key and lease your heart to me
The terms of the leasing agreement will be
forever and ever
I promise my love will be a good tenant.

It won't destroy any of your belongings
My love is the perfect tenant
It won't disrupt your life or keep you up at night
I assure you that my love is the right tenant.

It will be on time all the time
Take my hand, and I will show you love without
pain
Take my hand, and I'll never leave you out in
the rain.

Open

You may enter, sir
I am open like a door
Leave your baggage outside and please don't
dirty my floor.

Welcome
I am open
Open like a book
My cover may look amazing but don't judge me
by it.

Shawn Savoie

Most would think sugar and salt are the same
until they try it
Come inside
I am open
Open like a twenty-four-hour store
I have everything you need and more.

I welcome you into my world, but please don't
hurt me
I'm so afraid
Please don't hurt me.

The Voice Of Negativity

Stop looking out the window of imagination,
lady
You are only seeing things that will never
happen
That man will break you just like others
before him
His actions and words will partake in your
heartache.

Go ahead and let expectations take you high
So high that you feel like you can ride a cloud
and sail the winds
I shall be here when you fall because I have
always been there for you.

It is I who plant the seed of doubt in your head
in order to save you from the disappointment
of failure
You know love is very much like trouble
It's easy to get into but hard to get out of.

No matter how much you think you have grown
No matter where you go
I'll be right here whenever you need me
I am a true friend.

I have been in your life longer than any man
you've encountered, including your own daddy
You'll be back
I'll be waiting.

Learning All of Me

Sir, you probably thought the learning and tests
were over once you graduated college and high
school
I hope you realize that you're now enrolled in
my school.

You have to be all ears like an elephant
I'll tell you things about me and quiz you just to
see if you remember
Learning takes place from January to
December.

You could have had any chick you wanted, but
you chose the one with a broken wing
You could have been in anyone's atmosphere,
but you chose to be in my world.

You could have chosen anyone of God's
precious children, but you chose his most
stubborn daughter
Since you chose to be in my life, I need you to
know that I will not compromise.

You must change to fit inside my world
I will teach you how to love me
I will give you the blueprints of my temple
I will give you the key to my kingdom.

But, first, you must graduate from my school.

The Big Catch

Yes, there are plenty of fish in the sea
I can have any one of them, but I'm so into
mermaids
You're just that different, that extraordinary,
and that special.

I believe that when you bask in the sun, your
velvet skin absorbs rays that show in that bright
smile of yours
It's no wonder you have a smile that can light
up any room.

I'm not playing games, but if you are ever in a
playful mood, we can partake in a game of
twenty-one questions
I hope our game goes into overtime.

I want to learn everything about you
I want to get to know all three versions of you:
past, present, and future.

Self-Love

According to my ex, I was nagging him like
a bug
I had gotten so fat that if I emailed a picture of
myself, it would take forever to download.

He said my head was so big that it would take
me all day to look up
Whoever said words don't hurt must've had a
low comprehension.

Shawn Savoie

His words crumbled my pride and self-esteem
Like crackers in a child's fist
He called me his chick
Once I transformed into a beautiful dove
My ex flocked around to push and shove
himself back into my space.

He pays me attention, hoping I give him the
time of day in return
But, it's hours past concern, and I could care
less about what nice things he now has to say.

He hopes that I open up and let him in, but I'm
not up for a game of knock-knock
I don't care who's there.

I was a joke to him
I disgusted him
Now whether I'm in a dress with heels or
wedges
My curves and edges command his eyes.

I now realize that I always was and will be
beautiful
He broke me, hoping that no one could fix me
But I'm thankful that good men come with
good hands and good intentions.

Shawn Savoie

Here and Now

I heard you ask where I have been all your life
To tell the truth
I wasn't always the man that I am now.

I knew how to "Humpty Dumpty" your heart
back together because I once shattered hearts
I broke hearts just to see if love for me would
ooze out.

I drained people's energy like applications that
drain cell phone batteries
Thank God for change and growth.

Shawn Savoie

You asked
Where have I been all your life?
To be honest, I was making all the mistakes
that taught me to be the man a woman
deserves.

It's not about where I have been
It's about where I am at now
Just know and believe that you have the best
version of me so far.

My All

I'm not sure when was the last time you've
heard this, my lady, but my love for you is
immortal.
It's immortal like your favorite song
I want to make you so happy that your facial
muscles generate a smile that resembles the
letter U.

You're my all in all
To you, I give my all
All my time, all my love, and all my energy
All day, every day.

That means from dawn to noon, and long after
the sun changes shifts with the moon, it's all
about you
You will get all my time all the time
My affection will be smothering like southern
humidity.

I shall vandalize your body with hugs and
kisses
You inspire me to be the best man I can be
Like phones, you upgrade me to the best
version of myself.

Falling

Oh, how bittersweet falling in love is
It's not just a thing
It is a difficult process
It's never-ending progress.

The word falling alone scares me because I
have a fear of heights
You do actually have to fall before you love.

Fall and fall you must
Then trust that your special someone will catch
and keep you.
Hoping love will be in their actions, words,
eyes, hands, minds, and hearts.

Shawn Savoie

When love is one-sided, you will frown like
rainbows as the pain grows deep inside you
It will keep you up at night like a crying baby or
an upstairs neighbor who paces across the
floor with their heavy feet.

When the love is reciprocated, happiness will
look good on you
Everyone will compliment you on the way you
wear it
I swear it will illuminate those pretty eyes and
make your skin luster.

Don't be afraid to fall
Don't be afraid to love
Sometimes we have to experience the bad in
order to recognize something good.

I'm not happy that my man caught me because
I've been caught before
I am truly happy that he decided to keep me.

Caught

Us falling in love
Takes away my fear to fall
Thanks for catching me, dear.

Shawn Savoie

Battling Temptation

She plants seeds of lust in my mind and waters
them with temptation
My mental space gets littered with such filthy
images.

Like a snake, she's silent until she strikes
She doesn't attack when I'm strong
I know this
She comes when I'm at my lowest.

If I lose self-control, I also lose everything I
love and built
I'll be left with shame and guilt.

Shawn Savoie

Why does she spend her lifetime trying to
destroy things that were meant to last a
lifetime?
Like the air around us, she's forever present
She takes no days off.

Prayer pays off when it's hard to cope
On those days, I hang on to a thread of hope
Until I find the voice to tell temptation nope.

I will not be your victim
I refuse to be your slave
The war is never over
I know whether it's morning, noon, or night
I'll soon fight temptation.

Inseparable

I'm not sure if the other side of the sun is hot
I don't know why one plus one always equals
two, except when it comes to reproducing.

I can't tell you if there's gold at the end of the
rainbow
All I know is that I love you always and forever
Love is all I know.

God made me to love and with love
Your eyes are home to the most amazing light,
my lady.

Shawn Savoie

When I look at you
I know there is a God
I believe you were truly made in His image
Because I see parts of Him in you.

My goal is to be the best man you ever had
I want to give you a reason to look no further
In fact, the only thing you'll look for is your
mind because you will lose it once I plant
kisses on your lips.

I hope you know that whether it's swim or sink,
we will link forever and ever
No letting go.

I love you
You're always and forever in my heart
Take my hand
May nothing tear us apart.

Consistency

The same beautiful song plays as his love taps
on the drum of my heart
The same sugar rush hits me every time he
kisses me.

He still has the same love pulsing through his
veins
The same passion is in his voice when he talks
about us.

I notice how love and effort move him to
produce consistency
Consistency is his alter ego
Everywhere we go, it comes out of him.

Shawn Savoie

Like wine, this love gets better every day
We love each other in every way in every form.

When he doesn't feel like Superman
I'm his Superwoman
When I don't feel like Superwoman
He's my Superman.

Love In The Air

I truly love you so
I want the world to know
Every person, every creature, high and low.

I want him to tell them, and they will tell a bear
Then the bear will inform a dove that I fell in
love with an earth angel.

It's such a pleasure to lunge into your hugs that
are soft as a sponge
I often wondered how to find this area
This region we know as happiness.

Shawn Savoie

I'm so elated that you helped me find it
This is such beautiful weather; oh bless it be
It's raining; it's pouring; your love is all over me.

I gaze deeply into your eyes because I see the
great man you will be
Hopefully, you will see him too as time unravels
the future.

Loving you is the only way I know how to repay
you for pulling me out of the depths of
loneliness
So I will love you until the end of days
Until the sun no longer shines
Until it has no rays
I will love you, and that's forever and ever.

Never Ever Wonder

I love you with all of my heart, madame
There is no amount known to man that can
express how much love I have for you
But if I were to describe my love, I would say
it's heavy.

In fact, it's so heavy that, if I were to weigh it
The scale would read *one at a time, please.*

I can admit that I'm now a fan of Tasia
because when I see you, my heart jumps
across my chest cavity like rocks skipping on
water.

Oh, I wish I had the luck of the Irish
I hope lady luck makes me the luckiest man by
allowing this love to last forever.

I'm not a gambling man, but I know with you
I've hit the jackpot
I shall love you until evergreens lose their
pigment
I shall love you until the earth comes to a
standstill.

There is no amount known to man that can
express how much love I have for you
But if I were to describe my love for you, I
would say my love is deep like an ocean.

Every minute we're in it, we shall drift slowly,
just taking forever and a day to reach the
bottom of our endless love.

I See You

It's extremely hard not to notice your love,
my king
Your love is bright
It's as bright as a sunrise.

Your love is warm
It's as warm as a fireplace during winter
Your love feels amazing
It feels better than scratching an itch that
makes the eyes roll.

Your love is precious
I feel it in your kisses when you kiss me
I feel it in your hugs when you miss me.

Your love has wings
It is the reason I'm often taken to a higher
place
I just hate to come down.

This relationship is everything I hoped it
would be
Me loving you, and you loving me
I love the way you love.

The Power Of Love

I love you with every fiber of my being,
madame

I was drifting through life until you became my
anchor
I thank you for giving me a reason to smile
I don't know how you do this, but I drift in and
out of bliss with every kiss you plant on my lips.

To prove my love for you, I would go to Mars
and back
I would even bring stars back to show you that
you shine brighter.

Shawn Savoie

Your love is a drug, and it's hard to fight
the high
You have a smile that can light the sky
I wish your love was so embedded within the
fibers of my blanket so I can be reminded of
your hug.

May that blanket help me not to toss, turn, or
shrug as I sleep
I want to be everywhere you are
Whether you are far, near, here, or there
I want to share your air.

Put A Ring On It

There was a time when I wasn't worthy enough
to stand this close to you
You let your light shine upon me, and I stepped
into the shadows because I was afraid you
would see all my impurities.

Your love rained down on me and like sugar in
water
The stubborn man that I once was dissolved.

I am honored to call you my queen
Though this isn't checkers, you king me.
You bring me calmness in this world of
turbulence.

When I first asked your heavenly father for your
hand in marriage, he offered me a pair of wings
and said:
"It's not too late to run away."

I told him, this time, I'm running toward
something
So on bended knees, I am sending these words
to you: "Please marry me."

Yes, I know I should be on one knee, but I'm
on both knees because, like The Temptations,
I'm not too proud to beg.

When we started dating, my purpose was to
prove to you that
I wasn't wasting your time
If you say yes, my purpose will be to love you
for all time.
All you have to do is say "yes."

Confessions of a Queen

On many nights I trailed sleep into a dream
I dreamt of a man that loved to live and lived to
love me
I'm so elated that I no longer have to sleep in
order to see you.

You were patient enough to allow me to heal
You loved me enough to see beyond my scars
When you first found me, I was lost like a
needle in a haystack
I had forsaken love, but you helped me find my
way back.

Your love is extraordinary
The way you love has taught me that gifts and
romance don't end on February 15th
With you every day is Valentine's Day
I love you more than life itself
I must thank you.

Many men found me at my lowest and knocked
me down even further
You chose to lift me out of rock bottom.

I have to admit that sometimes I will be a
handful, but God isn't finished with me yet
I'm still under maintenance.

Soon we will give up our possessions
We'll let them go in order to obtain and create
something together
Something to call ours.

I choose to give my all to you for all time
I plan on proving to you that when a man finds
a wife, he finds a good thing
I will be your good thing.

Kindred Souls

This is outrageous, lady, but your love is
contagious, lady.

May it last for ages, lady
As I look at you, I sink into those gorgeous
eyes
I get lost
It feels as if we met in the past life.

Maybe you were my flower, and I was your bee
Or I was a fish, and you were my sea.

Shawn Savoie

We just couldn't live without each other
Your love is like a drug
With each hug and kiss, I submit to addiction.

I'm currently in the first stage, which is denial
When my friends all say you're making me soft
I deny it, but in the back of my mind, I know
you make my insides melt.

I just love the way you love
I've come to realize that love is a war
On this battlefield, I'm your sword and shield
You are my light.

We shall fight any opposition that tries to break
our union.

Touched By Love

My king
They say if you stand for nothing, you will fall
for anything
Once I decided to stand for love
I also fell in love.

Thanks for giving me the push I needed
I was drowning in fear until you became my
lifeguard
Gone are the days when I would say life's hard
I'm not sure what the future holds, but I hope
I'll be holding your hand.

Shawn Savoie

I hope this love never changes like evergreens
I've never seen myself glow this much
I shine like the other side of the sun.

This light of mine will shine for all to see
Love me forever and a day
Love me for all eternity.

Wedding Vows

My queen
My love
My confidant
When I look into your eyes, I see the world
from a better view
I see everything that's beautiful about it.

Everything in life is a choice, and love is no
exception
I choose to love you because you change me in
the best ways possible.

Shawn Savoie

When we first started dating, I was a good man
When we got engaged, I became a better man
I stand before today, a great man
That's how strong your love is
You are everything I want and need.

I hope by now you trust me enough
To share your troubles with me
Tell me your problems
I promise to let you solve them
I just want to help you get answers.

Let me join your battles
I'm ready and willing to fight for you and
with you
So far in my life, I have beaten negativity, bad
habits, doubt, and temptation
I'm no stranger to fighting.

Our story is no fairytale, but I'm glad we made
it to this page
This stage we call marriage
An older gentleman once gave me advice
about marriage
He said, "Happy wife, happy life."
I know you think you're happy now, but I've
only just begun.

I aim to make you so happy that your smile will
be visible to passengers on planes in the sky
I vow to love and cherish you, madame
Now, tomorrow, and forever.

Shawn Savoie

Vows of the Queen

I truly Erykah Badu need you, my king
Love of my life
My honey.

For us, love is a melody that makes us dance
like flickering flames
All praise be to the Almighty God for giving you
the vision to see the things that I could not.

When your eyes first gazed upon me, you saw a
work of art
When I looked at myself in the mirror, I saw a
piece of art that needed work.

It's amazing that I look nothing like the ugly
things I've been through
If I did, my reflection would be afraid to look
back at me.

I must also thank the Lord for giving you the
strength to lift the weight of the world off of my
shoulders.

On this very day
Togetherness will be confirmed through vows
and a kiss
We shall be one.

One voice
One action
One force.

God is the author of our love story, and we'll
illustrate by capturing moments inside photos
I vow to always be by your side until we reach
happily ever after
I will be here until the very end.

Honeymoon

Many footprints in the sand
Water and wind sweep the beach floor
Memories will stay.

Shawn Savoie

162

Summer Breeze

Warm and gentle breezes
They wake my nerves from slumber
Your kisses do the same.

Shawn Savoie

* * *

Pressure

Lady, you're the bomb indeed
You constantly blow my mind away
I find the way you move intriguing
Be not afraid as time ages the day.

We shall let thoughts play as self-control
flies away
We have candles and moonlight
If that's not enough light, the heavens created
a beetle that can harness light so that we can
witness the beauties of the night.

Shawn Savoie

We call them fireflies
Silhouettes from objects in the room dance on
the walls as the music plays
Every song seems to be about all the things we
long to do to each other.

No need for talking because, lady, I read you
I need you just as much as you need me
If your body is up for a discussion, we can
communicate through body language.

Picture That

I capture him
He captures me
Moments we hope to keep forever.

It's our insurance policy in case we get ripples
in our memory
With cameras, we capture seconds of love,
happiness, and perfection that will last always.

We both snap pictures of our serious, funny,
and off guard faces
Click, flash, snap.

Shawn Savoie

We seize each moment before we relocate to
the graveyard where we'll exist between a rock
and a hard place
These photos are more than memories
They are like words that combine to tell the tale
of our love.

No one will forget us and what we were
made of
Not us nor our family and friends
We shall capture so many images that our
minds and devices run out of storage.

Building Up

Oh, madame of mine
These hands of mine are at your disposal
Your every wish is my command
Whatever you demand, I will hand it to you on a
silver platter.

They're ready to construct your dream house
I'll decorate the walls with beautiful memories
I'll furnish the rooms with tender loving care
I'll make sure that we have our own bathroom
sinks.

You hate when I leave toothpaste in the
sink and
I hate when you leave hair in the sink
Let me assist you with starting your garden
Our love and happiness will grow as the
plants do.

Together there is nothing we can't do
Let my hands massage your pain away.

If you say, "Bring it on," these spirit fingers will
alleviate any pain
Whatever it takes to show my love and
appreciation, my hands will do it.

Summer Rain

The summer storm provides us with quality
time while it performs a symphony outside
Rain taps
Lightening snaps
Thunder claps
The electricity is out, but candles illuminate the
house.

Boredom and silence yell at us to do something
to pass the time
We pull out board games and cards
They seem to bring out our competitive side.

Shawn Savoie

We are two big kids trying to win a game so
that we can tease the other for being the loser
The children inside of us come out to play
We laugh, giggle, and boast.

When I'm near defeat
I make my husband retreat by threatening to
hold my kisses hostage
They are far sweeter than a victory.

Though the lights flicker back on
We continue to play because I'm in it to win it
This is a win that I plan to bring up in a lot of
our debates.

See-Food Diet

Maybe it's true that the way to a man's heart is
through his stomach
The first time I ate my wife's cooking, I was
hooked.

Her food was so good that I was ready to
forward all my mail to her place
I devoured everything she cooked
Her food is amazing.

Anything she cooks
I'll surely try it
She calls me greedy
I say I'm on a see-food diet.

Shawn Savoie

Sometimes I get so hungry
It sounds like my stomach is beatboxing
To speed up the process, I go into the kitchen
to see if my wife needs me.

She knows I'm trying to sneak a bite to eat
She kicks me out of the kitchen and threatens
not to feed me.

I just love my wife's cooking
I call it soul food
She puts something special inside of it
It changes my whole mood.

Soul To Soul

Subjecting

Ourselves to

Unconditional

Love that

Mobilizes

And

Touches our hearts

Everyday

Simultaneously.

Wet Dreams

Tell me, my lady
How does it feel?
I'm not trying to rock your boat
I'd rather row it because I know it feels so
much better if we take our time.

I want to love you the way a candle burns
Slow but steady
There is a place called crazy, and I'm going to
drive you there just so we can play out our
wildest fantasies.

Shawn Savoie

I hope you enjoy the ride
I shall hold your body until you fall fast asleep
Into a fantasy only we can keep.

I want to find your buried treasure
Let me dive into your pool of pleasure
And go so far no one can measure.

Please excuse these hands
This moment is for you and me
Let your lock invite my key, and we will unlock
feelings we never felt before.

I want to make your fountain overflow
And if your water falls, may it fall on me
Drip drop.

Sleepless

My dear sweet lady
I have the hard-to-snooze blues
We frequently play tug of war with the blanket,
but I constantly lose.

On cold nights I curl into the fetal position like
there is a pain in my tummy
Like a mummy, you're wrapped up tightly while
I shiver
I have the hard-to-snooze blues.

You say that you're not a terrible sleeper, but I
think you may be confused
You take up the entire bed
I'm forced to sleep in an awkward position that
leaves me sore
If you claim another inch of the bed, I'll be on
the floor.

I have the hard-to-snooze blues
It's when you want to stay up late to talk about
the news.

The conversation cannot wait until the morning
It doesn't matter how much I am yawning.

You complain about how I'm always tired
Sometimes you blow a fuse
I just want to watch the back of my eyelids
It's not my fault that I have the hard-to-snooze
blues.

I try not to start any type of argument, so I
listen to your stories
I listen to every word until sleep finds me.

Bun In The Oven

When my wife has cravings, she pouts and frowns
She eats anything that isn't nailed down
She says the baby needs food
Her belly starts to protrude
She's still my love though she's wider than a town.

Shawn Savoie

Bipolar Love

Sometimes, I want to be all under my husband
I just want to trade places with his shadow, so I
won't miss a moment with him.

I want to be a part of everything he's doing,
even if I'm not interested
When a basketball game is on, I celebrate
along with my husband whenever his team
scores a touchdown
Some mornings I hate for my husband to get
out of bed.

Shawn Savoie

Every five minutes, I ask for another five
minutes because it feels so good to be held
His arms are my favorite blanket
His chest is my favorite pillow
At times my husband aggravates me.

Sometimes I tell him that he can go back to
his mother because I can't raise a man
Other times, I tell him to just go whenever I
watch my favorite show.

Most of the time, I have to be right and have
the last word
Sometimes I say things I don't mean, like when
I say he gets on my nerves.

Or when I say he makes me sick and,
sometimes, when he asks where I'm going,
I reply by saying, "crazy"
I love my husband.

I'm glad he's strong and patient enough to deal
with all my personalities.

Sticks and Stones

Words have power
Big words
Small words
My words
All words.

I can look into your eyes and tell you that you're the most beautiful flower that has ever blossomed on this earth.

Then the skin around your mouth will start colliding, and your dimples will come out of hiding.

I just love that bright smile of yours
On the other hand, I could tell you that no one
cooks better than my mom.

Depending on how mad you are when we
get home
We will argue, or you will just knock me into
next week
But I wouldn't do such a thing because your
food is so good, my feet make a fist every time
I eat.

I love you, my lady
It's hard to imagine myself without you.

Even a minute away from you seems like
an hour
Since you're my flower, I shower you with love,
affection, and time.

This love is a rollercoaster that will face highs
and lows
But when happiness comes and goes
Hopefully, love stays to bond us through tough
days.

I shall think before I speak, knowing that words
have power
I will choose them wisely, my love
I'll think before I speak.

Shawn Savoie

Thorns

Women
They have been a pain in man's side since
Adam lost a rib
But we need them and love them.

Shawn Savoie

Happily Married

I love my husband
This feels heavenly
My angel is here with me
Prayers go to heaven.

I pray for a home that can house all the love
we have
Prayers go to heaven.

I pray that God will always be at the center of
my marriage
Prayers go to heaven.

Shawn Savoie

I pray God places a baby inside of my carriage
I hope he fills my womb with precious fruits
I hope we'll always be bonded in love and faith
Prayers go to heaven.

I pray that he and I will always be one
May God's will always be done.

Date Night

He dresses to kill, and I dress to steal all his
attention.

I'm the reason he puts his phone down
He compliments me all night
Instead of saying I look beautiful
My husband says I am beautiful inside and out.

We communicate using the five love languages
We spend quality time on date night
We can't keep our hands and lips off of each
other
He gives me cards and flowers.

Shawn Savoie

My hand never touches a door handle or knob
He reminds me why and how much he loves me
We drink, eat, laugh, and talk
Love is definitely in the air.

It's there, here, and all over the atmosphere
I wish I could put this night on repeat like my
favorite song
Everything is great, and as the night gets late
I plan our next date inside my head.

Beautiful

You are as beautiful as flowers displaying their
vibrant colors during the spring
You are as beautiful as a rainbow in the sky
after a summer rain.

You are as beautiful as a sunset when the sky
turns yellow, orange, blue, pink, and purple
You are as beautiful as a song that touches my
soul.

Beauty rest doesn't pertain to you, my queen
Because you're beautiful before you slumber
You are beautiful inside and out.

Such a beauty
My sun-kissed cutie.

They say that beauty is in the eyes of the
beholder
And these brown eyes of mine love capturing
images of your beautiful face.

Mommy To Be

Oh, child of mine
I really hope that my bad habits and mistakes
aren't hereditary.

I won't lie by saying I will give you the world
Instead, I will prepare you for the world.

Someday, I hope you find it in your heart to
forgive me for bringing you into this cruel
world.

Life is the hardest course you will go through,
but I promise
with each lesson learned, things will get easier.

To you, my child, I will give all my knowledge,
love, and energy
I know of a dream that doesn't require
sleeping
It only requires you to become a better person
than me.

I wish for you to inherit the strength of your
father
May it never allow fear to steal any of your time
and youth.

My child, I can't wait to meet you and greet you
with many hugs and kisses
I shall hug you so tight that my scent will seep
into your skin
For you, my child, I will be the personification
of love.

Love, oh love
Love will be in the air
Here, there, everywhere
In a few short months, you and I will share this
love.

Dear Unborn Child

To my unborn child, please bear with us
I'm trying to convince a woman who was never
taught how to be a mother that she will be the
best mother.

I'm trying to convince myself that I won't make
the same mistakes as my father
I can promise you that we will make mistakes.

I can also promise you that we won't treat you
like a mistake
As your mother and I go through our individual
battles, we'll undergo pain and scars in order to
hand you valuable wisdom.

We will shelter you with love, happiness,
patience, and guidance
Please be patient with us because, in life, every
day is a learning experience.

You'll teach us things, and we will teach you
things
Together we'll love, grow, and become better
versions of ourselves.

Family

It's a tree God plants
The parents are the strong roots
Kids are the sweet fruits.

Shawn Savoie

The Wait Is Over

The wait is finally over
Holding my bundle of joy feels surreal.

So precious and angelic
She has the warmest touch
So warm that it thaws the coldest hearts.

It's almost impossible to believe that
imperfections like us are capable of creating
something that's perfect in every way
It's as if we're magnetic.

Shawn Savoie

It's extremely hard to part from her
Her smile makes me take off my mask of
masculinity
She turns me into the biggest teddy bear.

I won't read her any fairy tales
I will tell her bedtime stories of a generational
curse and how she'll be the hero to break ours.

I want to be around for all of her first times
I especially want to be present for her first
word when she makes mommy mad by calling
for daddy.

Baby Fat

I wonder if I ask the mirror on the wall if I'm
the prettiest of them all
Will it be brutally honest, like my scale, by
showing me that I'm not where I want to be?

Maybe it will say I age gracefully like wine
Sometimes I envy the sun, and I have good
reasons to
It will always remain the same, but I will
change as the seasons do.

Shawn Savoie

Ripples in water remind me of imperfections
such as my stretch marks, flabby skin, and
wrinkles
I love that sweet man of mine
He still says that I am beautiful.

He has called me that over a million times, but
it doesn't feel as special as the first time.

Maybe he's being loving and nice
Maybe I'm overthinking
Maybe it's time to
Make a change.

Reassurance

Oh, how I love to be loved by thee
Thou art as beautiful as flowers, my Queen
I love you just the way you are.

Whether you're bigger or thinner
I will always love your outer and inner self
Victoria doesn't carry your size because you
have curves that not even Victoria can keep
secret.

Shawn Savoie

I love everything about you
Never forget that I fell in love with your heart
and soul
Beauty is only skin deep
Insecurity has no power if you can't hear her.

As you stand in the mirror, I need you to find
self-love and self-confidence
Whatever it is that you wish to change, I'll be
your biggest supporter just because I know
how important it is for you to be happy with
yourself.

I need to see you smile again
I have to hear you laugh again
I want you to be happy again.

I miss the old you
Way back when I told you that I could drive you
crazy, and then you said to me:
"Get back because I'm not ready to ride your
ride."

Loving and Learning Each Other

My husband
My king
My
Soulmate.

For us, love is an institution for the kindred
souls
We're two black butterflies that were destined
to be ever since we were caterpillars.

Maybe heaven paired us while we were in our
mother's cocoon
May our love grow out of control like wildfires.

In this institution of love, we majored in the
knowledge of each other
Once we graduated, we knew each other
mentally, physically, and spiritually.

I'm thankful for our change
I pray that we continue to grow and become
even better versions of ourselves.

I'm so happy that I taught you how to love me,
and I'm grateful that you taught me how to
love you
May we always flow through life together
Love will keep us flowing and gliding on our
journey.

Rainbow

To any queen that has ever had impurities
To any queen who is struggling with
insecurities
I know your pain; I was there too
We women have felt the type of pain that men
couldn't bear.

Stand tall and hold your head high
Your head shouldn't be down unless you've
dropped something.

Shawn Savoie

You are beautiful
You are enough
You are extraordinary
Embrace those curves.

Show the world that in jeans or a dress
You have more curves than the letter S.

Love the skin you're in
Dark skin, brown skin, yellow bone, redbone,
light skin, and not quite white skin
Such a broad spectrum of vibrant skin tones
and complexions
I like to believe that the rainbow inspired God
to create so many shades of beauty.

Only the color blind would say we all look alike
You look much better when you smile
Look up and never down
Readjust your crown
Strut and step, queen.

Living on Love

Oh my dear
You possess that lazy love
This is crazy, love, but you take my breath away.

As you wrap me in your arms
I wish that I could spend all day here
We could stay here and lay here while we drift
in and out of fantasy.

If your love were a drug, I would've overdosed a
long time ago
Your voice is music to my ears
You keep me in rhythm when I get the blues.

Shawn Savoie

Don't get confused when I say you sometimes
have me out of my mind
I promise it's not a bad thing
I'm just that crazy about you.

I'm not quite sure how you did it, but you
extracted me from reality and lightened my
heavy load
I feel light as a feather, lady
You could be the weather lady because you
have me walking on sunshine.

All I see are sunny skies and rainbows
You are more than a woman
On days when I don't feel super
You are there to be my hero, my warrior woman.

Kiss

I am sending you my love
I am blowing you a kiss, and I hope it makes it
to you
I hope the wind takes it to you
I hope when my kiss gets planted on you, it
makes your love for me grow out of control like
weeds.

I hope it lifts you up if you're down
May it cause you to smile and crack that angry
mask you sometimes wear on bad days.

Shawn Savoie

Sir, you have a smile that can make anyone
forget why they're mad
My kiss will brighten your day like the sun
It is sweeter than any source of sugar.

Bad News

Is there anyone who has ever been in my
shoes?
Is there anyone who has ever had to deliver
bad news?

How do I tell daddy's little girl that Daddy isn't
coming home?
How can I explain to her that heaven doesn't
have visiting hours or home passes?

I can picture us crying in bed as the pillow
collects our tears
She'll cry because she wants her daddy, and I'll
cry because I cannot stop her pain.

Shawn Savoie

I imagine that it will be hard for sleep to
subdue us, but hopefully, it comes to us and
brings peace
If only there were an exit door to help me
escape this horror for a brief moment.

To anyone who has ever had to carry out
this task
I just have to ask:
How do I tell daddy's little girl that Daddy isn't
coming home again?

Long Live the King

I know someone has heard the song that's
about pain, regret, and strife
It is called should've, could've, would've
The song is about my life.

My king, my love
The best parts of me died when you did
Without your love, my heart is like an acapella
performance
It has no beat.

Shawn Savoie

I should've never asked you to stop by the
store on your way home
I'm sure when you saw those lights flash in
your rearview
You were armed with your pride and rights.

Maybe the officers were intimidated by your
confidence and intelligence
I wish I were there to calm the situation
Just to convince you to do everything they say
So you could live to fight another day.

I should've been there to use my body to shield
you and blanket you with protection
If only that joke I told you long ago could've
been true
The one about you being so black that bullets
would need a flashlight to find you.

Maybe you wouldn't have been shot down like a
dog in the streets
I wish I had been there so I could tell your
truth.

I need you to know that I will fight for you
Fight for your name and fight for your image
I won't stop fighting until I find peace or until
the justice system crumbles into pieces,
whichever comes first.

Shawn Savoie

Pieces Of My Heart

Dealing with death is never easy
A part of me is broken
With each passing day, I see the fight in my
eyes dissolve like ice, and tears start to form.

You were the strongest person I ever knew
It's amazing that I still wear a smile
I guess your love is still able to reach me
I love you with every bit of my beating heart.

Shawn Savoie

As I escape reality to revisit the past
I ask myself why some things couldn't last
Time fading my memories is one thing that I
dread
So I etch them in my head constantly
I'm not ready to let you go.

I wish that time wasted was recycled by father
time to fabricate second chances
If only we had the chance to dance to our
favorite song
You would spin me around.

We would two-step
I step, you step
We would dance to the song
And dance to the song.

I know you're in a better place
When God came for you, I hoped he held you
because you always hated being cold
I hoped he closed your eyes because you were
a dreamer.

Long Gone

Forever thirty-one
Never to see thirty-two
You'll never see me
I'll never see you.

I truly hope that you're having a splendid time
in heaven
I wonder if you're witnessing Maya Angelou
and Bob Marley share poetry during their
afternoon talk
I wonder if Michael Jackson is teaching you
how to Moonwalk
If so, he has his work cut out for him because
you never had much rhythm.

Shawn Savoie

I'm not sad
I'm not angry
I'm not bitter
I'm just lonely.

I miss you as bad as Anthony Hamilton misses
his Charlene
I miss looking into your eyes and realizing
where stars go during the day.

Your absence created a lot of empty spaces in
my life
It's true that I can find any soul to love
But they could never be my mate
There is only one for me.

My Dear Diary

My dear diary
When paper and pen make their connection
My selection of words comes easy and eases
me when nothing else can please me.

I have things to say that not even walls can
keep secret
I saw another body drop today
They're killing us for no reason
It's open season on my people.

Shawn Savoie

Take and take
That's all they do
Take our lives, music, inventions, ideas,
freedom, and land
They want everything that makes us black
except our problems.

My dear sweet diary
All this killing subjects me to so much rage
We peacefully protest for change, but we are
handed the same violence.

We mothers have to say a prayer so long that it
doesn't end until our family returns home
Making it home was never promised to any
human being, but cops made black folks'
chances even slimmer.

I have to serve and protect my daughter
against those who swore to serve and
protect her
I am tired of turning the other cheek
Every cheek has been struck many times
already.

It's time they realize the black power fists are
for raising and for self-defense
Dear Diary, thanks for keeping my secret.

Shawn Savoie

Harsh Reality

Oh, that sweet child of mine
How can I tell her that she has a veil over her
eyes?
The veil makes her fearless.
It makes Christmas and birthdays magical
It makes her feel like she could be anything or
do anything.

She and I will face the world together
I want to be there when time and
responsibilities snatch that veil from her eyes.

Shawn Savoie

When trouble gets in her way, she will want
to weep
She'll close her eyes to forget, but demons will
be in her sleep.

My daughter will realize that in the real world
Villains aren't wolves, dragons, witches, or
giants
In the ugly real world, villains will be human
just like her.

The Power of Blackness

Oh, brothers and sisters
If only we would love each other
unconditionally
If only we weren't so materialistic
If only we would help each other out.

If only we weren't divided, we would have
enough black power to turn Wall Street into
Black Wall Street.

Every month would be Black history month
because February doesn't have enough days to
honor all those who fought and died for the
cause.

Shawn Savoie

The White House would be a museum to honor
the Black hands that built it
My dear brothers and sisters, when separated,
we are weak like rotten wood.

Together we are powerful like Muhammad Ali's
fists
If only every sister and brother in every
community would stand in unity, we would have
enough Black Power to implement the change
we want and need.

We Matter

Be not deceived people
Racism never ended
It was only suspended in the minds of
Americans, thanks to the media.

Be not deceived people
The KKK didn't fade away
They simply made a way to blend in with
society and move into law enforcement.

Their purpose is still to keep us in line, so keep
in mind that ignorance of the law is no excuse
Know the rules or face abuse.

Shawn Savoie

Be not deceived people
We all don't receive liberty and justice
It's just us that don't get our share of justice.

I wonder if everyone heard the chatter
They say all lives matter, but cops constantly
splatter the blood of my black folks
They expect us to be good ole boys and girls by
turning the other cheek.

So act like a coon and be so meek
By the end of the week, you won't get justice,
but at least you will know that this killing, too,
was another accident.

Every night and day, I pray
All this killing took my smile away
If heaven were a mile away, I would hide my
child away because the gates of heaven are
bulletproof.

Gratitude

Poetry is the exit door that allows me to escape my troubles for a brief moment. Every poem in this book is dear to me because each one is derived from actual events.

I'm thankful for the family and friends who encouraged me to share my poetry. Without them and God, my words would still be buried in the graveyard of my mind.

From the deepest depths of my heart, I thank you for reading my work. I hope the words in some of my poems jumped off the page and engaged in your thought process to heal, inspire, and uplift you.

I'm not quite sure when was the last time you heard this, but you are more than enough. I wish you love, peace, and happiness. Life is a transformational process. You should always strive to be a better version of yourself. Never give up.

You will go through difficult times but remember that you only go through them. God doesn't keep you there.

http://shawnsavoie.com

www.ingramcontent.com/pod-product-compliance
Lightning Source LLC
Chambersburg PA
CBHW061246210726
48293CB00003B/877